TIMELINES

1920s

by
Gail B. Stewart

CRESTWOOD HOUSE

New York

Library of Congress Cataloging In Publication Data
Stewart, Gail, 1949-
  1920s / by Gail B. Stewart.
  p. cm. — (Timelines)
  Includes index.
  Summary: History, trivia, and fun through photographs and articles present life
in the United States between 1920 and 1929.
  ISBN 0-89686-473-1
  1. United States—History—1919-1933—Juvenile literature. 2. History, Modern—
20th century—Juvenile literature. [1. United States—History—1919-1933—
Miscellanea.] I. Title. II. Title: Nineteen twenties. III. Series: Timelines (New York,
N.Y.)
  E784.S74   1989   973.91—dc20   89-34404
                                                             CIP
                                                             AC

Photo credits
Cover: The Bettmann Archive: Charles Lindbergh and the *Spirit of St. Louis*
Wide World Photos: 6, 10, 12, 14, 19, 21, 23, 24, 28, 29, 39, 40, 41, 43, 44, 45
FPG International: 8, 9, 11, 15, 25, 30, 33, 35, 36, 37, 38, 46
The Bettmann Archive: 4, 17, 20, 26

 Macmillan Publishing Company
866 Third Avenue
New York, NY 10022
Collier Macmillan Canada, Inc.

CRESTWOOD·HOUSE

Produced by Carnival Enterprises

Printed in the United States of America

First Edition

10   9   8   7   6   5   4   3   2   1

CONTENTS

INTRODUCTION

The 1920s are sometimes called "The Roaring Twenties." When World War I ended, people were relieved. The economy was doing well, and the world was at peace. People wanted to have fun. There were crazy dances, wild new fashions, and many new movies. It was an exciting time to be alive.

As the twenties progressed, however, problems began to emerge. Europe, it turned out, was not at peace at all. Powerful new dictators in Italy, Japan, Germany, and Russia vowed to fight no more. But World War I hadn't solved their differences and the political situation was still dangerous.

While some people were making fortunes, many others were just getting by. The average American worker earned $1,500 a year—for a 52-hour week. More and more people were feeling the bite of poverty. And as the 1920s ended, a monster raised its head—the Great Depression.

The newest dance craze of the twenties was the Charleston.

SHAME ON THE WHITE SOX

Is it true that baseball is the great American pastime? Maybe, but baseball took a real turn for the worse this year. The problem involved the Chicago White Sox, the winner of the 1919 pennant in the American League.

It was discovered that eight Chicago players had been betting against their own team in the World Series. To win their bet, of course, the White Sox would have to lose against Cincinnati.

In 1920, a grand jury accused these eight players of "throwing" the games. In other words, they played poorly so their own team would lose. Although there wasn't enough evidence to convict the players, they were banned forever from baseball. Known as the "Black Sox Scandal," this episode is still a source of shame for major league baseball.

"Shoeless" Joe Jackson was one of eight men accused of "throwing" the 1919 World Series.

NOT ON THE FARM ANY LONGER!

For the first time in its history, the United States could not call itself a rural nation. Until 1920, more than half of the population lived on farms. But the statistics in 1920 were surprising. Only 28 percent of the 105,750,000 people in America lived on farms.

OUT OF THE BLUE

The largest meteorite in history crashed to the earth in 1920. It fell in the southwestern part of Africa. Scientists estimated that the meteorite weighed more than 132,000 pounds!

TILDEN WINS AT WIMBLEDON!

No American man had ever won at Wimbledon—at least not until 1920. "Big Bill" Tilden became the first player from the United States to win the men's finals.

Tilden was famous for his blazing speed, as well as his serve. There were no machines in 1920 that could measure the speed of a serve, as there are now. But experts say Tilden's serve was as fast, if not faster, than that of anyone playing today.

BIRTH OF THE BAND-AID

In 1920, a man named Earle Dickson invented an item so important that almost every family in America keeps several in their medicine cabinet.

Dickson was a buyer for Johnson and Johnson, a company that made baby powder and gauze for bandaging wounds. His job was to find the best priced cotton for Johnson and Johnson's bandages.

1920

He got the idea for this item when he realized his wife frequently burned or cut herself while working around the house. Each time this happened Dickson took a piece of cotton and placed it over the wound. Then he held it in place with tape. Finally it dawned on him that he could make many of these bandages at once. That way, a fresh, clean bandage would be ready for the next burn or cut.

First he placed a small layer of cotton in the middle of a piece of tape. Then he put stiff linen over the sticky part of the tape to keep it from losing its glue.

The idea worked! When he showed his bosses at Johnson and Johnson what he had invented, they decided to produce and sell the ready-made bandages. Earle Dickson was a hero.

Women walked from New York to Washington in a rally for voting rights.

The 19th Amendment finally gave women the right to vote.

WOMEN FINALLY HAVE THEIR SAY

In November, Republican Warren G. Harding was elected president of the United States. Harding and his running mate, Calvin Coolidge, won easily over the Democratic ticket of James Cox and Franklin Roosevelt.

This election was important in another way. It was the first national election in which women could vote!

9

LOW MARKS FOR U.S. TEACHERS

In 1921, people were worried about the conditions of American schools. Overcrowded classrooms, poor materials, and unqualified teachers were blamed for the problems.

Teachers were not as well trained as they are today. In 1921 there were about 600,000 teachers in the United States. Of those, 30,000 had never gone beyond the eighth grade themselves! Teachers were also quite young. Almost 20 percent of America's teachers were under 21 years old.

HONORING THE NATION'S UNKNOWN SOLDIERS

Two years after World War I, the U. S. government still had a debt to pay to some special American soldiers. These were the people killed in the war whose bodies had never been identified. As a result, their families and friends had never been notified of their deaths, and the soldiers had never been honored with funerals. Instead, they had been buried anonymously in a war cemetery in France.

The casket of the Unknown Soldier passes through Washington on its way to Arlington National Cemetery.

The Memorial Amphitheater was built to house the Tomb of the Unknowns.

In 1921, the government asked Edward Younger to choose one of the soldiers' caskets to be brought back to America. Edward Younger had received more medals and honors than any enlisted man in World War I. The soldier he selected was buried in a special tomb in Arlington National Cemetery in Arlington, Virginia, to represent all the unidentified Americans who had died in World War I.

Watched over by a select honor guard, today the Tomb of the Unknowns contains bodies of unknown soldiers from three more wars—World War II, the Korean War, and the war in Vietnam. On the tomb are written these words:

> *Here Rests in Honored Glory*
> *an American Soldier known*
> *But to God.*

11

THERE SHE IS!

The first Miss America Beauty Pageant was held in 1921. This was, and is today, a contest to choose "the most beautiful girl in America." The first winner was Margaret Gorman, from Washington, D.C.

MASTERING A HARD GAME

José Capablanca learned to play chess when he was four years old. Without any help at all, he figured out how to play the complicated game by watching his father. He shyly asked his father if he might play, too. His father laughed and said that he could try.

Sixteen-year-old Margaret Gorman (second from the left) was the first Miss America.

José won. His father was astonished. Perhaps, he thought, the first win was a fluke. They played again, and again José beat his father!

That's when José's father realized that his son had a rare talent. The two played a lot together, and José improved every day. When he was 12, José beat the champion of Cuba, where he lived, and became the national champion! People who hadn't taken him seriously before were now impressed. He was asked to participate in matches all over the world.

In 1921, Capablanca became world champion. When asked whether he read a lot about chess, José said no, he played by instinct. Instinct was more important than brains, he said.

THE COOK WHO NEVER WAS

The Washburn Crosby Company, which made baking products, was in trouble. It was receiving a lot of letters from customers asking advice on baking and cooking problems, but all it had was an impersonal business executive to answer them.

Finally, someone in the company suggested that they reply to the letters under a made-up name. The name should sound warm and trustworthy—a name like Betty.

That idea appealed to the president of the company. To complete the name, they decided to use the last name of their recently retired director—William Crocker. From then on, all letters from the company about baking tips were signed "Betty Crocker."

In 1921, they held a contest within the company to find a signature that looked trustworthy. A secretary won.

"Betty Crocker" became so well known that eventually Washburn Crosby decided to use her name not just on letters but on their baking products as well. Her signature—the one penned by the secretary in 1921—still is used on all their products today.

INJUSTICE DONE TO A GREAT AMERICAN

The son of a black slave, George Washington Carver grew up thirsty for knowledge. At the time, it was against the law to teach a black child to read and write.

But he wasn't about to let such prejudice stand in his way. He grew up to be a great scientist. He used his specialty—botany, the study of plants—to help farmers in the South.

At the time, southern farmers had grown mostly cotton in their fields. But cotton took a lot out of the soil. After years of being planted with cotton, the soil no longer contained nutrients to grow good crops.

Carver convinced the farmers that by changing their crops to peanuts or sweet potatoes, they could put nutrients back into their soil. His ideas changed farming forever and meant millions of dollars worth of profits for southern farmers.

Despite all that Carver had contributed to his country, he was still treated as a second-class citizen. In 1922, after speaking to Congress about his ideas on farming, he was refused service in a white restaurant. To many, the color of his skin was more important than the contributions he had made to the American people.

Dr. George Washington Carver at work in his laboratory at Tuskegee Institute

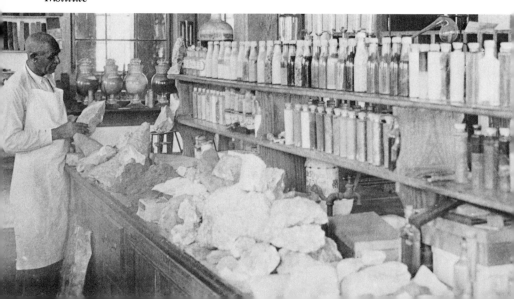

George Washington Carver meets with Edsel Ford.

A FAMOUS COMBINATION

Peanut butter was invented in 1890 by a doctor from St. Louis, Missouri. But it wasn't until the 1920s that peanut butter and jelly became a popular sandwich. Among the under-12 age group, it was the most asked-for sandwich in 1922.

NEW MAGAZINE TAKES OFF

In 1922, a young man from St. Paul, Minnesota, named DeWitt Wallace realized that many Americans were too busy to keep informed about the world around them. People just didn't have the time to read everything they should.

Wallace decided to start his own magazine, with shortened versions of important articles from other magazines. That way, the public would have to read only the main points of each article. He called it the *Reader's Digest,* and it sold like hotcakes!

The first issue was published in February 1922. There were 1,500 subscribers that first year. Today the circulation has ballooned to more than 15 million!

DEADEYE

In March, a woman named Annie Oakley made newspaper headlines all over the country. For years, she had been a star of Buffalo Bill's Wild West Show.

But in 1922, people learned that Oakley was more than a cowgirl in a colorful costume. She was a sharpshooter who broke every record the sport had ever had. One of those records was broken at the Pinehurst Gun Club in North Carolina, where she won the Women's Trapshooting Competition. Oakley, who first began sharpshooting at age eight, hit 98 targets out of a possible 100.

THERE SHE IS, AGAIN

In 1922, organizers of the Miss America Beauty Pageant decided they needed new rules. The most important, it seems, was that perfume and scented makeup should be banned. Rumor had it that the lovely smells of some of the contestants had unfairly swayed a few of the judges.

Starting in 1922, the only sweet smells allowed in the contest would come from the flowers each girl carried.

PLEASE AND THANK YOU

The number one book on the bestseller list in 1922 was not an adventure story or a mystery. It was a little book about manners, written by a woman named Emily Post.

There had been lots of other manners, or etiquette, books written. But for some reason, this one became a classic. Many people say that Emily Post's book was different because it was not snobbish.

Whatever the reason, Emily Post is still the number one name in questions of good manners!

Annie Oakley

1923

SINGING THE BLUES

The first recording of the blues was made in February 1923. A form of jazz noted for its sad, mournful sound, blues singing was popular in nightclubs. Bessie Smith, a black woman from Chattanooga, Tennessee, was the recording artist. People around the country flocked to buy Smith's record. The record included the songs "Tain't Nobody's Business If I Do" and "Downhearted Blues."

DAY BY DAY, IN EVERY WAY

Couism, a way of curing depression and other ills, was hot news in 1923. The founder of Couism was Emile Coué, a French chemist. His idea was that if you said something over and over, you could change the way you felt or thought.

His favorite saying was "Day by day, in every way, I'm getting better and better." A firm believer in self-suggestion, Coué maintained that a sick person who repeated that sentence over and over, hundreds of times a day, would begin to feel much better.

His critics called him a quack and his ideas ridiculous. His supporters were loyal. They claimed Couism cured everything from gallbladder problems to seasickness.

ONLY A SUPERSTITION?

The ancient pharaohs of Egypt were buried with precious gold and jewels in secret tombs. It was said that anyone who disturbed the tomb of a pharaoh would be cursed and die soon after!

In 1922 Lord Carnarvon, a famous archaeologist, and Howard Carter discovered the 3,000-year-old tomb of King Tutankhamen. It was one of the most important finds in history, revealing countless priceless objects—many of solid gold.

But the rumors about the pharaohs' curse were whispered everywhere. What would happen to Lord Carnarvon and his as-

18

Four years after the discovery of King Tutankhamen's tomb, Howard Carter continued to study the king's treasures.

sociates? In April 1923, less than six months after opening the tomb, Lord Carnarvon died of an insect bite. He had received the bite while working in the tomb. It became infected, and he died of blood poisoning.

MILTON WINS INDY

A St. Paul, Minnesota, driver named Tommy Milton won the Indianapolis 500 race on May 30. Milton averaged almost 91 miles per hour. He collected $35,000 for his efforts!

19

TERROR AND THE KKK

The Ku Klux Klan (KKK) is a terrorist organization that believes whites are superior to other races. In the 1920s, the Klan openly tortured and killed many black and Native American citizens.

Angered because the Klan was so powerful, Oklahoma Governor J. C. Walton tried to do something about it. In 1923, he declared martial law, under which U. S. soldiers could be used to keep peace.

But the legislature in Oklahoma refused to let Governor Walton declare martial law. Instead, they suspended him as governor.

Members of the Ku Klux Klan march the streets in a suburb of New York City.

A dance marathon gets under way in California.

PUT ON YOUR DANCING SHOES

One of the crazes of 1923 was the dance marathon. In this contest, couples danced as long as they possibly could without stopping. Some marathons went on for as long as 45 hours.

But authorities, including police departments around the country, were concerned. Many of the dancers were in bad shape as they staggered off the dance floor. Swollen ankles, bad backs, and bleeding feet were just some of the complaints. Should these contests be outlawed? When one woman went into convulsions after losing 21 pounds on the dance floor, officials said "Enough!" They decided to let the courts in each state decide if these contests should be illegal.

THE NATION MOURNS THE DEATH OF A PRESIDENT

President Warren G. Harding died on August 2, 1923. Weakened by a trip to Alaska, he developed pneumonia. At first, he seemed to be recovering. Then one day as his wife was reading to him, the president had a severe stroke. He died immediately.

Vice-president Calvin Coolidge was sworn in as the 30th president of the United States.

GERSHWIN HYPNOTIZES AUDIENCE

George Gershwin's *Rhapsody in Blue* was premiered on February 12, 1924. A highly original mixture of classical form and jazz chords, *Rhapsody in Blue* became an immediate hit.

Gershwin performed the music with the famous Paul Whiteman orchestra. The concert took place in New York City.

CALVIN COOLIDGE, JR., DIES

The son of President Calvin Coolidge died on July 7, 1924. He had cut his foot while playing tennis a few days before. When he later complained of severe stomach pains, he was taken to the hospital. The cut had become infected, and Calvin Coolidge, Jr., had blood poisoning. Although doctors and nurses tried hard to save him, the poisoning proved deadly.

MONSTER SIGHTINGS IN THE WOODS

Bigfoot, or Sasquatch, as the Native Americans called it, was said to be a frightening sight. The creature was between 7 and 12 feet tall and weighed between 600 and 900 pounds. It looked a little like an ape and walked on two feet.

For centuries various Native American tribes had told about coming face to face with the creature. And since 1811, settlers and explorers in Washington, Oregon, and parts of Canada had also reported seeing it. But one of the most famous brushes with Bigfoot occurred in 1924.

A young man named Albert Ostman said he had seen Bigfoot while on a camping trip. He had awakened during the night and found, to his horror, that he was being carried—sleeping bag and all—by a giant creature.

The creature carried him deeper into the forest, to a den where a family of four Bigfoot creatures lived. Ostman said he was terrified: Even the smallest of the creatures could have killed him. He said they kept him in their den for almost a week before he was able to escape.

FIRST WINTER OLYMPICS HELD

Never before had the Olympics been a winter event. Although a few winter activities had been included in the Olympics, the January 1924 Olympics was the first to feature all winter sports.

The first Winter Olympics took place in Chamonix, France. Most of the medals were won by athletes from the Scandinavian countries. The United States did bring home one gold medal, however, thanks to a speed skater named Charlie Jetraw.

American Olympic representatives march through opening ceremonies in Chamonix, France.

Ku Klux Klansmen march in Washington, D.C.

KLAN'S MEMBERSHIP AT ALL-TIME HIGH

The Ku Klux Klan, an organization dedicated to hating Catholics, Jews, blacks, and anyone else who isn't white Protestant American, was very strong in 1924. An official count put its membership at four million that year—far more than at any other time in history.

We tend to think of the Klan as operating mainly in the South. But in 1924 many of its members lived in the Midwest. In fact, Indiana had more Klan members than any other state in the nation that year.

24

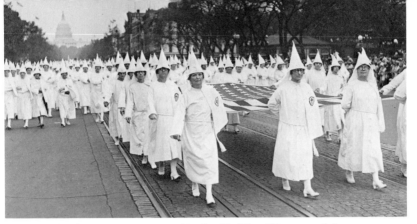

Thousands of women participated in the Ku Klux Klan march in Washington, D.C.

RICH BOYS COMMIT MURDER FOR THRILLS

When a 14-year-old boy, Bobby Franks, disappeared one afternoon as he was walking home from school, the police assumed he had been kidnapped. Since his father was a millionaire, everyone waited for the kidnappers to demand ransom for the boy.

But Bobby Franks wasn't being held for ransom. He had been beaten and strangled to death. The police found a pair of eyeglasses near his body. This clue led police to arrest Nathan Leopold, Jr., and Richard Loeb, two 19-year-olds. Both were also sons of millionaires. Leopold and Loeb confessed to killing Bobby Franks. They had no real motive, they said, except "for the thrill of it."

Leopold and Loeb were sentenced to life in prison.

"ME FOR MA"

On November 4, the first woman governor in the United States was elected in Texas. Miriam Ferguson went by the nickname "Ma." The banners in her campaign proclaimed "Me For Ma" in big letters.

25

POOH'S BEST FRIEND

Almost every child has heard of Christopher Robin. He and his friends Winnie the Pooh, Piglet, Eeyore, and the rest are the subjects of many stories. But did you know that Christopher Robin was a real boy?

His full name is Christopher Robin Milne, and the stories were written by his father, A. A. Milne. In 1925, Christopher was five years old.

That's when Christopher's father published his first best-selling book, *When We Were Very Young.* Over the next several years he wrote *Winnie the Pooh, Now We Are Six,* and *The House at Pooh Corner.*

When he was young, Christopher liked the fact that his father put him in his books and that so many children enjoyed reading about him and his stuffed animals. But as Christopher got older, he got teased quite a bit. He wanted people to think of him not as a skinny boy with boots on, but as a real person with feelings.

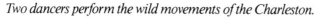

Two dancers perform the wild movements of the Charleston.

"UP ON YOUR HEELS, DOWN ON YOUR TOES"

A new dance craze was sweeping the nation in 1925. It was called the Charleston, named after the city in South Carolina where it started.

The Charleston was a fast dance that involved lots of swinging of arms and legs, while the dancer kept his or her toes pointed inward.

One of the steps many people enjoyed was done standing still. The dancers put their hands on their knees and opened and closed their knees. It looked as though their knees had crossed from behind!

C2-559

It's hard to believe, but in 1925 a dog began serving a term in prison. The convict was a black labrador retriever from Pennsylvania named Pep, and in 1925 he was sentenced to life in prison!

Pep was usually a good dog. However, late in 1924, he chased and killed a cat. The cat, it turned out, belonged to Pennsylvania Governor Gifford Pinchot.

Mrs. Pinchot was angry. She demanded that her husband go next door and shoot Pep. The governor got police to lock the dog up instead.

A trial was held, and poor Pep was found guilty. (He reportedly had no lawyer.) Pep was handed over to the warden of a state prison in Philadelphia and, like every other inmate, Pep was given a number. His was C2-559. He was assigned a cell block and was very popular with the other prisoners. In the morning after roll call, the men assigned to building a new prison nearby were called by number by the warden. Pep got to know his number and jumped on the prison bus whenever he heard it announced!

Pep spent six years in prison before dying of old age.

VARIETY OF COLORS

In 1925, automaker Henry Ford made the unprecedented decision to paint his cars in colors as well as in black. A buyer, he announced, now could get a gunmetal blue, highland green, phoenix brown, or fawn gray Ford, as well as the classic black.

THE MONKEY TRIAL

In March 1925, the Tennessee State Legislature passed a famous law. The law stated it was illegal for a school to teach about creation in a way that contradicted the Bible. This law was aimed against those who believed in the theory of evolution, Charles Darwin's idea that humans were descended from monkeys in the animal kingdom.

John Scopes (right) talks with John Kia, one of his lawyers.

Clarence Darrow (left) and William Jennings Bryan at the Scopes Monkey Trial.

Later in 1925, a teacher named John Scopes was accused of breaking that law. He supposedly taught his high school science class about Darwin's theories. He was arrested and tried.

The trial, called by the press the "Scopes Monkey Trial," received a great deal of publicity. A lawyer named Clarence Darrow defended John Scopes. William Jennings Bryan, who had run for president three times, was the prosecutor. Emotions ran high. It seemed everyone in America had a strong opinion about the case.

Scopes was found guilty as charged and was fined $100.

1926

DEATH OF A MASTER MAGICIAN

Harry Houdini, perhaps the most famous magician in the world, died in 1926 on Halloween night. Houdini, who began performing at the age of nine, was best known for his amazing escapes.

Over the years he escaped from bank vaults, boxes made of iron, and all kinds of handcuffs. He always said his secret wasn't really magic at all. He had learned, he said, to use every muscle in his body. He used his toes as nimbly as if they were fingers.

Ironically, the end came when he was speaking to a college class in Canada. He was explaining how solid his stomach muscles were and how he could make his abdomen as hard as a rock. Without warning, a student jumped up and hit him three times

Harry Houdini and his wife, Wilhelmina

30

in the stomach. The student didn't know it, nor did Houdini, but the punches ruptured the magician's appendix. By the time Houdini sought a doctor's help, it was too late.

A FAITHFUL DOG

After hearing and reading so many stories about faithful dogs who would do anything for their masters, most of us wonder sometimes if the stories are ever true. Could a dog really be that loyal?

A man in Japan owned a little dog that loved him very much. Every morning the man would walk to the train, which took him back and forth to his job in the city. The dog, whose name was Hachi, followed along beside his master every morning. And at exactly 5 P.M., when the train returned, Hachi was there to greet him.

One day in 1926 the man wasn't on the 5 P.M. train. Hachi waited and waited, but the man didn't appear. He had died in the city, but, of course, Hachi didn't understand. Puzzled, the dog walked home. The next day, Hachi tried again.

Neighbors fed the dog and were friendly to him. But every day, for the next ten years, Hachi walked to the station and met the 5 P.M. train. When he died, the government put up a statue of Hachi on the spot where he always waited.

FLYING OVER THE WORLD

On May 9, 1926, two men successfully flew over the North Pole. They were the first to dare to fly over the top of the earth.

The fliers were Commander Richard E. Byrd and Floyd Bennett, both Americans.

They began their flight in a Fokker tri-motor airplane just off the coast of Norway. It took 16 hours to overfly the pole, turn around, and return to their starting place.

31

1926

ROCKET MAN

Known as the father of rocketry, Dr. Robert Goddard developed many of the principles on which rocket flight is based.

In 1926, when he was visiting his aunt's farm in Auburn, Massachusetts, Goddard launched the world's first rocket powered by liquid fuel.

Eighteen years earlier, he had predicted that people would be able to fly to the moon. He also had drawn up plans for aircraft that could fly unmanned and rockets powered by hydrogen and oxygen. Unfortunately, his ideas were so far ahead of his time that people often laughed at him. Today it is clear that Goddard was a genius.

SWIMMING ACROSS THE CHANNEL

On August 6, Gertrude Ederle swam across the cold, choppy English Channel. She was the first woman ever to do so. She accomplished this feat in 14 hours and 31 minutes. Although several men had swum the Channel before, none had done it in such good time.

A 19-year-old from New York, Ederle had tried once before unsuccessfully, in 1925. But this time she was determined not to let anything stop her. She walked into the water at Cape Gris-Nez, France, and vowed not to stop until she came to the coast of England.

Reporters and friends followed in a small boat. At several points in the swim, they begged her to stop. The cold winds and large waves seemed to be getting the best of her. But she ignored their pleas and kept on swimming.

She was met by British officials, who jokingly demanded to see her passport before allowing her to come ashore.

32 *Gertrude Ederle with her trainer a few days before she swam across the English Channel*

UPS AND DOWNS

In 1927, Donald Duncan saw a toy that fascinated him. It went up and down, and twirled like a "potato on a string."

The toy, Duncan learned, was called a yo-yo and was brought to the United States from the Philippines by a man named Pedro Flores. Flores carved his yo-yos out of wood and painted them bright colors.

The more Donald Duncan saw of Flores's yo-yos, the better he liked them. He bought the company Flores had started and the rights to use the name "yo-yo." He sold his first product under the name "O-Boy Yo-Yo Top." To interest kids in the toy, he hired people to travel from town to town doing tricks with their yo-yos. These experts would teach kids some basics and then organize contests and tournaments. The yo-yos were a huge success.

As the years passed, many improvements were made on the first yo-yo. Yo-yos were built to hum and glow in the dark; they were painted with cartoon characters. But the basic idea is the same as the "potato on a string" that Duncan first saw in 1927!

CANDY BARS CAUSE TRAFFIC JAM

The Baby Ruth candy bar was invented in 1927. But it was *not,* as many people think, named after Babe Ruth the baseball player! It was named after President Grover Cleveland's little daughter.

The candy was a mixture of fudge, peanuts, and caramel. The price was a nickel. To call people's attention to the new product, the manufacturer decided to drop hundreds and hundreds of the candy bars from an airplane flying over the city of Pittsburgh. The "flying candy" produced the same reaction then as it would today: People stopped to swoop them up! Traffic was delayed more than two hours, police reported.

A young boy performs the Top Drop, one of the tricks kids could do with their yo-yos.

1927

THE HERO OF THE DECADE

It took him more than 33 hours, but Charles Lindbergh from Minnesota did it. He did what no other pilot had done. He flew nonstop across the Atlantic Ocean, from New York to Paris!

Like many other fliers, Lindbergh was interested in a $25,000 prize that had been offered to the first person to accomplish this feat. He helped design the plane for this long flight and called it *The Spirit of St. Louis,* in honor of his financial backers.

Lindbergh's plane was loaded with gasoline and just managed to get airborne when it took off from Long Island. Since there was no possibility of stopping for fuel, it was important that the plane had all the gasoline it could hold.

Lindbergh was greeted by more than 100,000 shouting people as he landed in Paris on May 21, 1927.

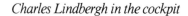

Charles Lindbergh in the cockpit

The Spirit of St. Louis

BABE RUTH SETS A NEW RECORD!

Babe Ruth, the slugger for the New York Yankees, set a new world's record on September 30. Facing a left-handed Boston pitcher named Thomas Zachary, the Babe belted out his 60th home run of the season.

AN EPSICLE?

In 1927, a man named Frank Epperson unknowingly invented a great treat. He was a lemonade salesman who accidentally left a glass half full of lemonade on a windowsill. The weather turned cold that night. The lemonade, with a spoon stuck in it, froze solid.

Epperson was no fool. He realized right away what a great dessert this frozen juice was. He froze more, this time with a wooden stick in it. Delicious!

Proud of his invention and eager to get credit for it, he named it the Epsicle. It wasn't renamed the Popsicle for years. But the name didn't really seem to matter. Everyone who tried an Epsicle loved it.

Sonja Henie

15-YEAR-OLD WONDER

One of the brightest stars at the 1928 Winter Olympics was a 15-year-old girl named Sonja Henie. A native Norwegian, Henie won a gold medal in figure skating.

What set Henie off from the others was her dramatic way of skating. She got into the music, as an actress gets into a difficult role. She also amazed judges by new spins and tricks that hadn't been done before.

Often, Olympic stars vanish from the public eye after the games are over, but not Henie. She went on to win more World Championships and two more gold medals in the 1932 and 1936 Winter Olympics. After that, she moved to the United States and starred in ice shows as well as movies.

AN EXCITING BROADCAST

On January 4, 1928, radio listeners in all 48 states got a real thrill. The Dodge Motor Company sponsored a live radio broadcast starring performers in different cities.

The first performer was the famous humorist Will Rogers, speaking from his home in Beverly Hills, California. He delivered part of his monologue in Spanish for the benefit of the Mexican people listening.

The Paul Whiteman Orchestra performed from New York. From New Orleans came singer Al Jolson. Fred and Dorothy Stone sang from Chicago.

TRAGEDY IN CALIFORNIA

On March 13, the St. Francis Dam broke. The dam, which was part of the Los Angeles water supply, let loose more than 12 billion gallons of water, flooding the Santa Clara River Valley and San Francisquito Canyon.

The catastrophe occurred early in the morning. There was no warning at all. Hundreds of people were reported missing. The final death toll was 400.

Witnesses to the dam's collapse said there was "a towering wall of water, maybe 80 or 90 feet high." Torrents of water washed away roads, farms, cattle, and people.

After its collapse, only one wall remained of the St. Francis Dam.

COLOR MOVIES FIRST APPEAR

In July camera maker George Eastman showed off some new technology—color movies! For the first time, it was possible to film moving pictures in color, and the impact on Hollywood was tremendous.

The pictures Eastman showed in 1928, however, had no plots or suspense. He showed viewers films of goldfish, flowers, and colorful birds.

WOMAN FLIES ACROSS ATLANTIC

On June 18, Amelia Earhart became the first female passenger on a flight across the Atlantic Ocean. Earhart flew in a Fokker plane named *Friendship*. She told people that she wasn't trying to prove how brave she was. She merely wanted to demonstrate how safe and easy flying was. Long flights such as this one, she predicted, would be common in the future.

Amelia Earhart with Wilmer Stulz (left) and Louis Gordon (right), her co-pilots in her flight across the Atlantic.

Stan Laurel (middle) and Oliver Hardy (right) look bewildered as a man demolishes a player piano in The Music Box.

STAN AND OLLIE

The hottest comedians in the movies were two men who couldn't have looked less alike! Stan Laurel and Oliver Hardy burst onto the scene in 1926. By 1928 the duo had made ten movies.

Their charm was their bumbling slapstick. Laurel got upset and whimpered. Hardy continued to flick his necktie and giggle. No one has yet put a finger on what made them so unbelievably funny—but it doesn't matter. Audiences in 1928 (and every year since) just couldn't get enough of Laurel and Hardy.

HOOVER ELECTED

Republican Herbert C. Hoover beat New York Governor Al Smith in the presidential election on November 7. Hoover had 444 electoral votes to Democrat Smith's 87. Smith was a Catholic, and a candidate's religion was important to voters. The first Catholic president, John F. Kennedy, was not elected until 32 years later.

"FATHER OF FROZEN FOOD"

Clarence Birdseye owned a little company that he sold in 1929. The buyer was the Postum Company, which later became General Foods. Birdseye earned $22 million on the deal. What was it that made the Birdseye Company so valuable? Frozen vegetables!

Birdseye came up with the idea when he and his family were living in northeastern Canada, where the weather was almost always cold. Birdseye found that food could be kept fresh by plunging it into icy water. When the water froze, the food froze, too. After doing hundreds of experiments with all types of vegetables and meats, he brought his ideas back to the United States.

When he sold his company, the new owners agreed to keep the name "Birdseye." In fact, they kind of liked it, although they did split it into two words.

DEATH OF A LEGEND

On January 13, Wyatt Earp died at the age of 80. He had become the most famous lawman of the American West when he took over the job of marshal in Dodge City, Kansas. In a time when there were as many corrupt lawmen as there were reliable ones, Earp was dedicated and honest.

FAMOUS BOY SCOUT

Ever since the Boy Scouts of America had been established in 1910, many of America's presidents had become honorary scouts, and were proud of it. But in 1929, there was a slight switch. A boy joined a scout troop who would grow up to be president!

John Kennedy was the boy's name. He joined Troop 2 in Bronxville, New York. He was active in the troop until 1931. He was the first active scout to become president.

ST. VALENTINE'S DAY MASSACRE

On February 14—Valentine's Day—a bloody crime occurred in Chicago. Seven members of underworld figure Bugs Moran's gang were lined up against a garage wall and shot. The killings took place near a wealthy Chicago neighborhood.

It was reported that some of the killers were impersonating police officers. Police began looking for Al Capone, whose gang was thought to be responsible.

The St. Valentine's Day Massacre

Buddy Rogers (left) and Richard Arlen starred in Wings, *the first movie to win an Oscar.*

THE FIRST OSCARS

In an effort to make the movie industry more respectable, the first Academy Awards were presented in 1929. The award was a gold-plated statue of a man stabbing a film reel with a sword.

Supposedly the statue had no name until one of the secretaries in the Academy office was unpacking the first ones. "He looks just like my Uncle Oscar," she exclaimed. The nickname stuck. Today people call the statues "Oscars."

The first year, the best picture Oscar went to *Wings,* a silent film, as were all the nominees.

BLACK THURSDAY

Thursday, October 24, was a horrible day for America. Many people had been buying stocks in various companies. Everything was fine for a while. Stock prices got higher and higher. Business in America was booming.

44

But on this day, there were rumors of stock prices dropping. Suddenly, people were afraid to hold on to stocks whose worth was declining. No one wanted to lose money.

So, they rushed to sell the stocks. On October 29, more than 16 million shares were sold at low prices. For example, some stocks, which the day before had sold for $100, were dumped for $3 on Black Thursday.

Whole fortunes were completely wiped out, and there were many reports of people killing themselves. President Hoover tried to assure the American people that there was no reason for alarm. He predicted the stock market would swing up again, and prices would be as they had been. But not many believed him. Historians today see Black Thursday as the beginning of the Great Depression.

1929

Mounted police keep people moving past the New York Stock Exchange Building (second building from the right) after the market crash.

BROOKLYN DAILY EAGLE

And Complete Long Island News

LATE NEWS
WALL STREET
★ ★

NEW YORK CITY, THURSDAY, OCTOBER 24, 1929

WALL ST. IN PANIC AS STOCKS CRASH

Attempt Made to Kill Italy's Crown Prince

STOCKS CRASH IN RUSH TO SELL; BILLIONS LOST

ASSASSIN CAUGHT IN BRUSSELS MOB; PRINCE UNHURT

Hollywood Fire Destroys Films Worth Millions

FEAR 52 PERISHED IN LAKE MICHIGAN; FERRY IS MISSING

PIECE OF PLANE LIKE DITEMAN'S IS FOUND AT SEA

High Duty Group Gave $700,000 to Coolidge Drive

CARNEGIE CHARGE OF PAID ATHLETES ROUSES COLLEGES

HOOVER'S TRAIN HALTED BY AUTO PLACED ON RAILS

WARDER SOUGHT TO KEEP SEA TRIP SECRET, AID SAYS

SOMERS NAMED AS HEAD OF NEW EXCHANGE BANK

Today's News

DANCERS IN PANIC AS MAN IS STABBED; POLICE SEIZE 5 MEN

Mae Murray Suit Asks $250,000 for Foot Hurt

10 ARABS SENTENCED TO LIFE TERMS FOR PALESTINE MASSACRE

DOG TALKIE STAR KEEPS SILENCE IN AUTO STORE WRECK

Two Are Held in Bail As Speakeasy Owners

THE EAGLE INDEX

The "Roaring Twenties" came to an abrupt halt with the crash of the stock market in 1929.

46

INDEX

48